過來，戴西！
Come on, Daisy!

Jane Simmons

Chinese translation by David Tsai

MILET

To my Mum

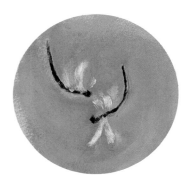

Come on, Daisy! / English-Chinese

Milet Publishing Limited
PO Box 9916, London W14 OGS, England
Email: orders@milet.com
Web site: www.milet.com

First English-Chinese dual language edition published by Milet Limited in 2000
First English edition published by Orchard Books, London in 1998

Printed in Singapore

"戴西，你必須靠得近一些。" 鴨媽媽說道。
"我會的。" 戴西答道。

"You must stay close, Daisy," said Mamma Duck.
"I'll try," said Daisy.

可是戴西並沒有靠近。
"快過來，戴西！" 鴨媽媽喊道。

But Daisy didn't.
"Come on, Daisy!" called Mamma Duck.

但戴西卻在那兒看魚。

But Daisy was watching the fish.

"趕快過來，戴西！" 鴨媽媽又一次喊道。
可是戴西卻在遠處追趕蜻蜓。

"Come on, Daisy!" shouted
Mamma Duck again.
But Daisy was far away chasing
dragonflies.

"到這邊來，戴西！" 鴨媽媽大聲地叫道。
可是戴西卻在睡蓮葉上蹦來跳去。
啊，真是快活極了。□，□！

"Come here, Daisy!" shouted Mamma Duck.
But Daisy was bouncing on the lily pads.
Bouncy, bouncy, bouncy. Bong, bong!

"撲通！"是一隻青蛙。"啊..."戴西輕輕地嘆道。
"呱，呱..."青蛙叫著。

"Plop!" went a frog. "Coo..." said Daisy.
"Gribbit," said the frog.

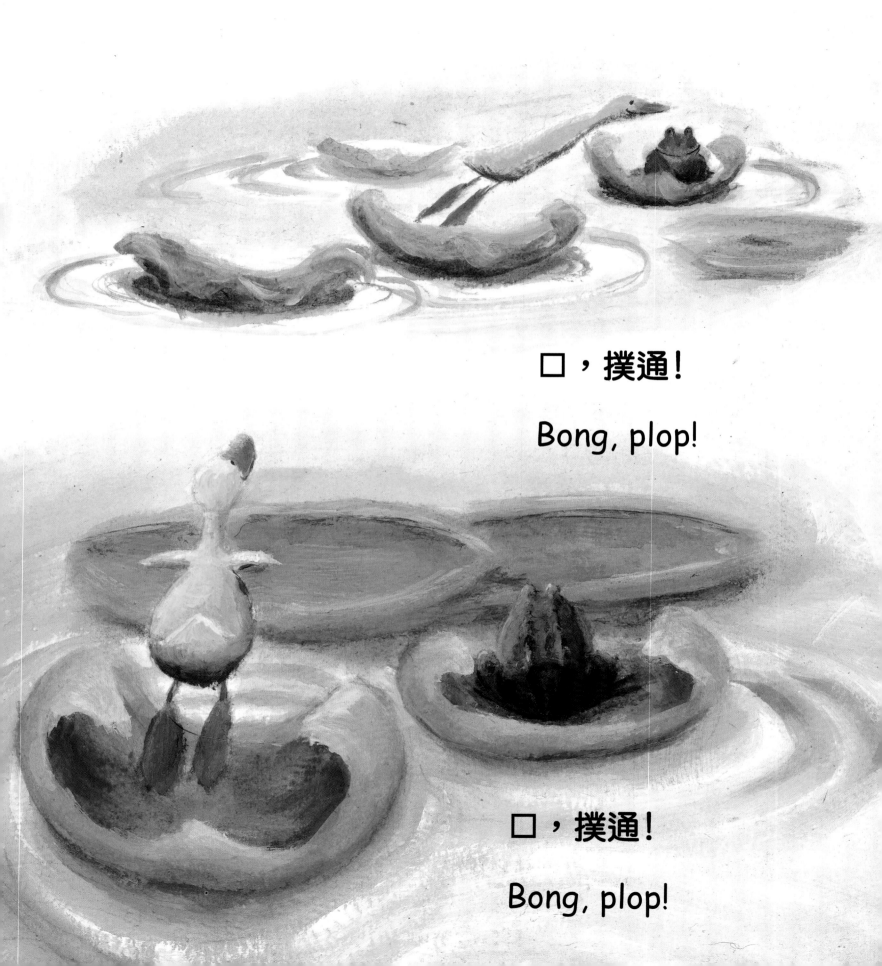

口，撲通！

Bong, plop!

口，撲通！

Bong, plop!

□，撲通！

Bong, plop!

咕咚！

Splosh!

"請過來吧!" 戴西說道,可是青蛙已經不見了。

"媽媽!" 戴西喊著,但鴨媽媽也已經不見了。

只有戴西一個人留在那兒。

"Coo!" said Daisy, but the frog had gone.

"Mamma," called Daisy, but Mamma Duck had gone.

Daisy was all alone.

有個大東西在她身下攪動，
戴西嚇得直發抖。

Something big stirred underneath her.
Daisy shivered.

她趕緊爬上了河岸。
可是，從上空卻傳來了尖叫聲！

She scrambled up on to the riverbank.
Then something screeched in the sky above!

所以，戴西便藏進了蘆葦叢中。
要是媽媽在這兒該多好啊！

So Daisy hid in the reeds. If only Mamma Duck was here.

河岸邊傳來了沙沙聲。
戴西可以聽到這聲音越
來越近⋯

Something was
rustling along the
riverbank.
Daisy could hear
it getting closer...

...越來越近，

越來越近，

越來越近...

...and closer,

and closer,

and...

CLOSER...

是媽媽!
"戴西，快過來!" 她說道。戴西立刻照辦。

It was Mamma!
"Daisy, come on!" she said. And Daisy did.

雖然她又跟蝴蝶在一起玩耍…

And even though she played
with the butterflies...

但她卻緊緊地呆在媽媽的身邊。

she stayed very close to Mamma Duck.